Michael in Motion!

The Bike Ride Guide

by Kristin Smedley
illustrated by Kim Crothers

PICTURE WINDOW BOOKS
a capstone imprint

Published by Picture Window Books, an imprint of Capstone
1710 Roe Crest Drive, North Mankato, Minnesota 56003
capstonepub.com

Copyright © 2026 by Capstone. All rights reserved. No part of this publication may be reproduced in whole or in part, or stored in a retrieval system, or transmitted in any form or by any means, electronic, mechanical, photocopying, recording, or otherwise, without written permission of the publisher.

Library of Congress Cataloging-in-Publication Data is available
on the Library of Congress website.
ISBN: 9780756588823 (hardcover)
ISBN: 9780756588878 (paperback)
ISBN: 9780756588861 (ebook PDF)

Designed by Jaime Willems

An ebook edition with audio narration is available. Visit capstonepub.com/librarians/ebooks for more information.

Words to Know

balance—to keep steady and not fall over

blind—not being able to see with your eyes

Braille—a system of writing where the letters are represented by raised dots that can be felt to read

cane—a tool used to help someone walk independently; some visually impaired people use a white cane

driveway—a private road that goes from the street to a house or garage

TABLE OF CONTENTS

Chapter 1
All Clear!...8

Chapter 2
Bike Buddies...14

Chapter 3
Guide on the Ride...20

Meet Michael

Michael loves music. He sings and plays piano. He also loves playing and watching sports. Baseball is his favorite. He loves being outside too.

Michael is blind. He does not see with his eyes. He uses his tools of blindness to do all the things he wants to do.

Michael uses a white cane to confidently walk on his own. He uses glasses to see bits of light and shapes more clearly. He wears sunglasses outside. He uses Braille to read.

Braille

Braille is a series of dots that make up letters and words. Look at each letter and the dot pattern that goes with it.

In a Braille book, every dot is raised so you can feel it. Then you can read with your fingers.

Aa	Bb	Cc	Dd
Ee	Ff	Gg	Hh
Ii	Jj	Kk	Ll
Mm	Nn	Oo	Pp
Qq	Rr	Ss	Tt
Uu	Vv	Ww	Xx
	Yy	Zz	

Chapter 1
All Clear!

"Great walk, Daisy," Michael says.

He reaches out and feels for a hook on the wall. It's where he always hangs his white cane.

Michael uses the cane to walk safely because he is blind. He does not see with his eyes.

Then he feels for another hook and hangs Daisy's leash on it. Now everything is in its place.

Michael can hear his mom typing in her office.

"Can I go for a bike ride?" he asks.

"Sure. Don't forget to wear your helmet," she replies.

Michael gives Daisy a hug. "I'm going for a bike ride, Daisy. You stay inside with Mom."

Michael gets his cane and puts it in front of him. Then he heads to the garage.

Michael walks through the garage to his bike. It's always in the same spot. He hangs up his cane and feels for his bike.

He feels the cool metal under his fingers and smiles. Then he finds his helmet on the shelf above the bike and puts it on. He's ready to ride!

Chapter 2
Bike Buddies

Michael walks the bike onto the driveway and climbs on. He listens for cars or people nearby. He only hears Daisy barking.

"All clear!" Michael yells as he takes off.

Michael feels the wind against his face. He pushes the pedals harder as he races down the long driveway.

"Wheee!" he yells.

Michael feels the bike ride over a small bump. That means he's at the end of the driveway. He turns around and races back.

"Wheee!" he yells again.

Michael's younger sister, Karissa, is waiting for him. Daisy is waiting too.

"That looks like fun," Karissa says. "I'm too afraid to ride my bike."

"What are you afraid of?" asks Michael.

"That I won't be able to stop!" she exclaims.

"You just have to use your brakes. I can show you," Michael replies.

Michael and Karissa walk Daisy inside. Michael feels for the hooks. He hangs up his cane and Daisy's leash. He can hear his mom filling a glass of water in the kitchen.

"Can I help Karissa ride her bike?" he asks.

"Sure. Wear your helmets," his mom replies.

"We will!" they say together.

Chapter 3
Guide on the Ride

Karissa grabs her helmet and bike. She has tried to ride a bike before. She knows how to balance. She knows how to pedal. But she's scared she will fall.

Karissa gets on her bike. Then she gets back off. She gets on again. Then she gets back off again.

"You can do it. I'll be the guide by your side," Michael says.

Karissa takes a deep breath and gets on her bike. She pedals slowly.

"Keep going," Michael says.

Karissa pedals faster. Michael is right by her.

"Now push back on the pedals and brake," he says.

Karissa pushes a little too hard. She slowly tips over into the grass.

"Well, that wasn't supposed to happen," Karissa says, laughing.

Michael laughs too.

"Let's try this again," Karissa says.

"You can do it!" Michael cheers.

Karissa pedals faster this time.

"Brake!" Michael yells.

Karissa brakes. This time, she doesn't fall over.

"I did it!" she yells.

Michael and Karissa keep going. Up and down the driveway. Over and over. They have so much fun they lose track of time.

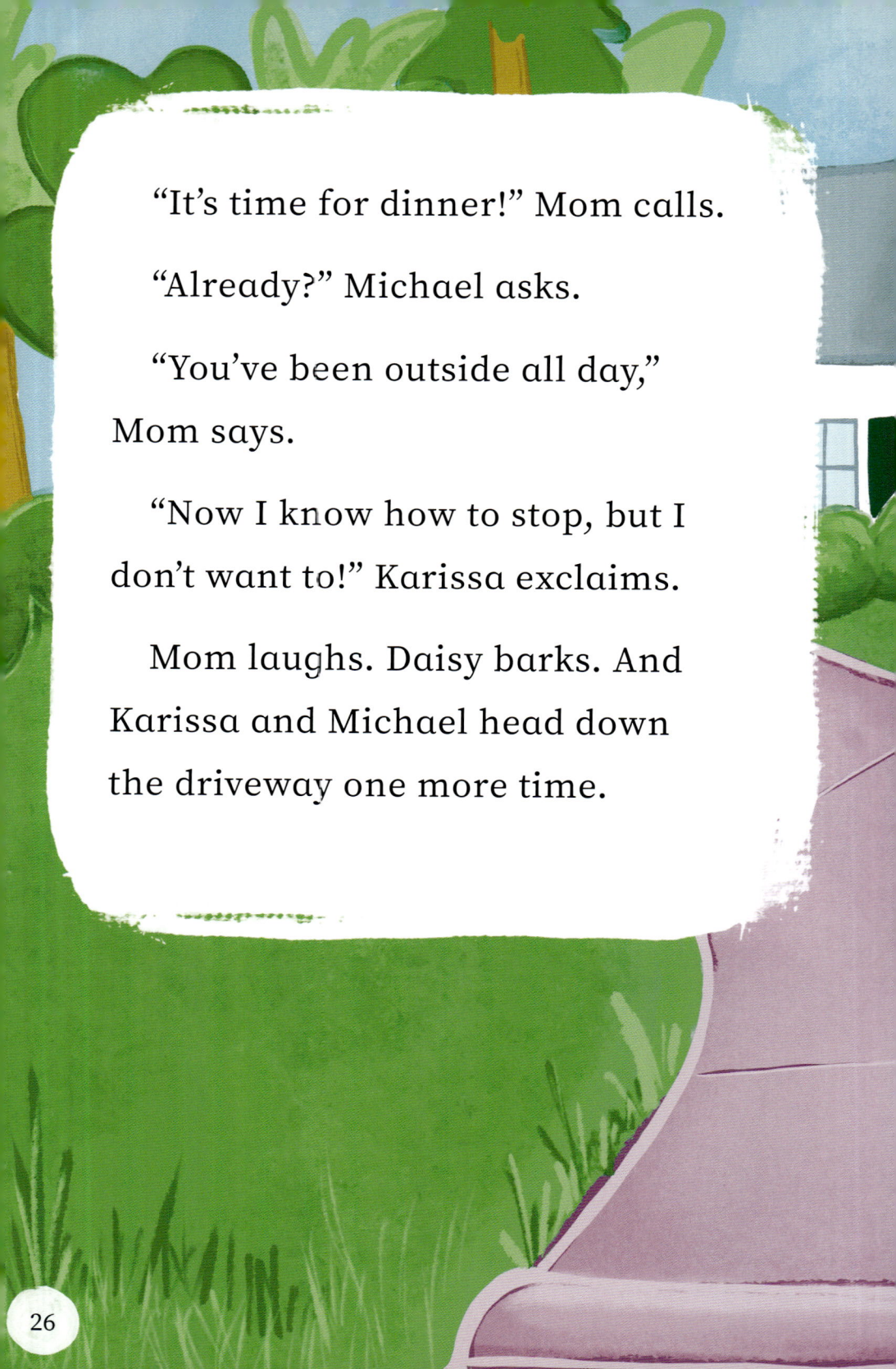

"It's time for dinner!" Mom calls.

"Already?" Michael asks.

"You've been outside all day," Mom says.

"Now I know how to stop, but I don't want to!" Karissa exclaims.

Mom laughs. Daisy barks. And Karissa and Michael head down the driveway one more time.

More About Michael

This story is based on the life of the author's oldest son, Michael. He learned to ride a bike when he was 5 years old.

Before getting on the bike, he listened to directions. He asked questions. He wanted to understand how the bike worked.

After learning everything he could, Michael put on his helmet and got on his bike. He listened to the sounds around him.

Then he took off and rode down the driveway. His great balance helped. So did his confidence.

Michael still loves to ride bike. He also likes to ride a tandem bike with his mom or a friend in parks and in cycling events.

Left to right: Karissa, Mitchell (Michael's brother), Kristin, and Michael

How Kim Creates

At 6 years old, Kim Crothers was diagnosed with a rare eye disease. Autosomal Dominant Optic Atrophy (ADOA) causes her to have low vision and color blindness.

A love of art led Kim to pursue her degree in graphic design at Mississippi State University. This set up her career as a freelance illustrator, artist, and graphic designer.

When Kim isn't drawing, she spends time with her husband, three kids, three dogs, and her parents in Madison, Mississippi.

Do you like working on the computer or using traditional methods to draw?

I like a mixture of both! When I'm drawing on paper, I use a thick black marker. It's easier for my eyes to see bold lines than thin lines.

I often digitize my drawings and add detail and color on my computer. I also create digital brushes from traditional art.

My computer and digital tablet have a tool that allows me to zoom in on my drawings so I don't miss details. Since everything is bigger, I can use a wider variety of pencils, brushes, and markers too.

Kim can zoom in on her digital tablet to draw smaller details.

Think and Share

1. Were you surprised that Michael was the one to help Karissa learn to ride? Why or why not?

2. Michael and Karissa used many bike safety rules. Look back in the story and find at least two things they did to stay safe.

3. Think about riding a bike. What does Michael have to do differently than you to ride?

About the Author

Kristin Smedley is a TEDx speaker, award-winning author, trailblazer for the disability community, and mother of three children, two of whom were born blind.

Kristin is a cofounder and CEO of the only patient organization in the world for people living with the rare eye disease CRB1 LCA/RP, which caused her two sons' blindness. She also cofounded Thriving Blind Academy.

Kristin lives in Pennsylvania, where she works endlessly to teach others how to move past their fears and obstacles to achieve their dreams.